and the Fountain of Happiness

TRICIA SPRINGSTUBB

illustrated by

ELIZA WHEELER

CANDLEWICK PRESS

Text copyright © 2015 by Tricia Springstubb
Illustrations copyright © 2015 by Eliza Wheeler

First paperback edition 2016

Library of Congress Catalog Card Number 2014945449
ISBN 978-0-7636-5857-1 (hardcover)
ISBN 978-0-7636-8753-3 (paperback)

19 20 21 22 23 TRC 10 9 8 7

Printed in Eagan, MN, U.S.A.

This book was typeset in Dante.
The illustrations were done in ink and watercolor.

Candlewick Press
99 Dover Street
Somerville, Massachusetts 02144

visit us at www.candlewick.com

CODY

and the Fountain of Happiness

Books about Cody

Cody and the Fountain of Happiness

Cody and the Mysteries of the Universe

Cody and the Rules of Life

Cody and the Heart of a Champion

1
Today!

In this life, many things are beautiful:

Marshmallows

100% on your spelling test

Turtles, with their cute thumb-shaped heads

But if Cody had to name the most beautiful thing in the world, it would be . . .

The first day of summer vacation.

Which was today.

Today!

The sun shone and the birds sang. Cody was making toast when her mother came click-click-clicking into the kitchen. On her feet were sea-green pumps with silver buckles. They were just the kind of shoes a mermaid would wear, if mermaids had feet.

Wearing gorgeous shoes was Mom's job. She was a shoe salesperson at O'Becker Department Store.

"You're already up!" Mom said.

"I don't plan to waste one minute of vacation," said Cody.

Mom nodded. She hated wasting time, too. *Click-click-click* (her shoes). *Gulp-gulp-gulp* (her coffee).

"Too bad camp doesn't start till next week," she said.

Camp! The word was a dark cloud on a bright day. Camp was hikes in the boiling sun and swim lessons in freezing water. Last year, Cody had almost died of thirst because she refused to drink bug juice. Bug juice! The name was an insult to insects across the land.

But Mom and Dad believed camp was a good environment, so what could Cody do? In this life, grown-ups hold all the power. It has been that way since ancient times.

"I'm a little worried about leaving you with Wyatt." Mom's forehead did its folding-fan imitation.

Wyatt was Cody's big brother. He was a teenager who pretended that Cody drove him crazy. Wyatt was so good at pretending, many people were fooled. But not Cody.

"I'll take care of Wyatt," Cody said. "Promise."

Mom and Cody hugged good-bye, and then *click-click-click,* Mom was out the door. Uh-oh. *Click-click-click.* Mom was back in the door.

"Remember, no screen time before five," she said. "And no turning on the stove. Or bringing ants into the house."

"I know very well," said Cody.

"Good-bye!"

"Good-bye!"

Cody practiced eating toast with her right hand. Though she was left-handed, one of her goals was to be ambidextrous. In an emergency, being able to use either hand could come in handy. Handy! Cody cracked herself up.

Afterward, she took the crusts outside to feed the ants. Cody loved all animals, big and small. But she had a special, tender place in her heart for ants. They were so serious! They worked so hard! She watched them bubble up out of their tiny ant volcano. They picked up toast crumbs and dragged them inside. A few crawled over her big toe. This was ant for "Thank you."

If only every day could be this wonderful!
Nothing to do.
No one telling you to hurry up or slow down.
Nothing to do.
No one telling you to speak up or quiet down.
Nothing to do.
Hmmm.

By now most of the ants had disappeared. Cody imagined them underground, having a giant toast feast together.

A tiny bit lonesome, that's how she began to feel. But she knew how to fix that.

Time to wake up good old Wyatt.

2
Brain Pain

Wyatt possessed many talents:

Speaking Spanish for real, not fake

Giving headlocks even Houdini could not escape

Eating an entire box of cereal in ten minutes (Cody held the stopwatch)

But his *número uno* talent was sleeping. If people let him, he could probably sleep for a hundred years, easy.

Good thing Cody was an expert on waking him up.

First, she perched on his invisible bed. No one had seen the actual bed in years. It was like Earth, with its many layers. Only in place of an outer crust, the bed had T-shirts and underwear and dirty dishes and books.

Wyatt loved to read. He was so smart, you could practically hear his brain whirring inside his skull. Even when he was asleep.

But wait. That wasn't his brain. It was his iPod. Very gently, Cody pulled out an earbud. She whispered, "There is a tarantula on your arm."

Wyatt just rolled over.

Cody tickled his feet.

She sang "You Are My Sunshine."

On and on he slept. He was so talented!

At last Cody stood by the window.

"What do you know?" she said in a voice of surprise. "Payton Underwood is coming up our front walk."

Payton Underwood was the girl of Wyatt's

dreams. He had been in love with her forever, but Payton didn't love him back. How could it be? In this life, there are many mysteries.

"Waaa?" Wyatt rocketed to life. He tried to leap out of bed, but his feet got tangled in the sheets. Underwear flew. A dirty dish went into orbit. Wyatt

landed on his back. His arms and legs paddled the air like a beetle that can't flip over.

"Oh, wait," said Cody. "I guess it was the mailman instead."

Wyatt stopped moving.

Now Cody felt terrible. Terrible for tricking him. Terrible for Payton Underwood not loving him back. Quick-quick, she had to cheer her brother back up.

"It's the first day of vacation, *amigo!*" she said. "Just you and me, all day long!"

Wyatt moaned softly.

"Want to go to the dog park and pick what dog we'd get if only we were allowed to get a dog?"

Wyatt put his hands over his eyes.

"No?" said Cody. "How about we look for rocks and have a rock stand and use the money to buy a skateboard?"

Wyatt slowly got to his feet. He was very tall and skinny. If he were a building, he'd be a skyscraper, but a droopy one.

"*Silencio,*" he said. He toppled back into bed and

pulled the covers over his head. "You are causing me pain. A big fat pain in my cerebral cortex."

"Do you want some tea?"

"No, Brain Pain. I want you to disappear. Preferably forever."

"I can't," said Cody. "I promised Mom to take care of you. I never break a promise."

"Let me go back to sleep, or something else will get broken."

Cody waited awhile. Lately, Wyatt could be in a rotten mood one minute and a superb one the next.

But the lump of covers didn't move. Cody's shoulders sagged. This wasn't how the first day of vacation was supposed to go. She plucked a T-shirt off the invisible bed and pulled it over her clothes. The shirt was black, with a picture of an exploding alien robot. It smelled like Wyatt's anti-pimple soap. Next she selected a fat book with a boring cover.

"I'm stealing your stuff," she said.

The lump did not reply.

Dragging her feet, she crossed the room, but at the door, she stopped. Everyone deserves another chance. Cody believed that.

But Wyatt said not a word. Feeling sad, Cody left the room.

3
To the Rescue

It was a hot day. The ants were off on business. Cody sat on the front steps and opened Wyatt's book.

"'The lining of the gut replaces itself every three days,'" she read. "Eee-yoo. What is that supposed to mean?"

Too bad the book had no gut picture. Cody was a good reader, but she appreciated pictures. Especially of interesting things like guts.

"MewMew! MewMew, where are you?"

A boy a little bit younger than her walked slowly

by. His round head swiveled from side to side. When he saw Cody, he stopped.

"Have you seen a striped gray cat?" he asked. "Kind of fat? Fourteen and a half years old?"

"That's how old my brother is!" Cody slapped her book shut and stood up.

"And she's deaf," said the boy.

"Deaf! Then why are you calling her?"

The boy's glasses were smudged, but Cody could still see how sad his eyes were.

"It makes me feel better to say her name." *Blink-blink* went his eyes. "She's my grandma's cat, and she's not allowed out. But I let her. Just for a minute. To keep me company. But something scared her and she ran away!"

There is a certain kind of sadness that belongs to somebody else, but feels like it belongs to you too. Cody felt that sadness now.

"We'll find your cat," she promised.

They walked to the end of the street, but no MewMew. Just as they turned the corner, Cody heard something. She cupped her fingers behind her ears, making them stick out. Wyatt had taught her this trick to catch extra sound waves.

Up in a tall pine tree, a furry snake swayed back and forth among the needles.

"I found her!" yelled Cody.

"MewMew!" The boy held out his arms. "You're saved! Come to Spencer!"

But MewMew didn't move.

"Maybe you need to talk slower," said Cody. "So she can lip-read."

"Come. To. Spencer."

"You. Are. Saved."

That didn't work. Neither did trying to climb the tree. Cody ran home, grabbed a jug of milk, and ran all the way back. She waved it around under the tree, but MewMew was not interested.

By now Cody was very hot, so she drank some of the milk herself.

"What are we going to do?" Spencer balled his hands into fists and dug them into his cheeks. This was not a fun thing to watch. "It's all my fault!"

"As long as we're here, nothing can happen to her." Cody sat down under the tree. "Cats don't live in trees. She has to come down sometime."

Spencer sat beside her.

"I wish I had a cat or a dog," Cody told him. "But my brother is allergic. So instead I have ants."

"Ants aren't pets." Spencer made a face of disgust. "Ants are pests."

"An ant can lift an object that weighs a thousand times more than it does!"

"Are you sure about that?" Spencer pushed his glasses up onto the bridge of his nose and looked at her.

Cody wasn't *exactly* sure, but sure enough.

"Also, when one ant meets another ant, they rub feelers to say hello. They are extremely friendly." Cody put extra oomph into those last two words. In her opinion, Spencer had some work to do in the friendly department.

"At home I have rare and valuable tropical fish," he said. "Our neighbor is feeding them while I'm here."

"What about your parents?"

"They went on a vacation. They have their own business and they work twenty-four/seven and they

needed a grown-up getaway." Spencer took off his glasses. Without them, his face looked naked as a baby bird.

"Do you wish you went, too?"

Uh-oh. Wrong question.

"I love Grandma Grace," Spencer burst out. "But I really miss Dad and Mommy!"

A small pain stabbed Cody's heart. Her dad was a trucker. He was gone for days at a time, and even though she knew he would come back, she always missed him, especially at night. Poor Spencer. Cody scrounged her brain for a cheerful thought.

"The lining of your gut replaces itself every three days!" she said.

"You act like you know everything," he said.

"That is a very rude comment." Cody stood up. "I promised to find your cat, and I did. Now I will be on my way." She dusted her hands together.

Mew mew! Mew mew!

They both looked up. MewMew was inching down the tree. Headfirst. Her paws scrabbled on the bark, trying to keep a grip. A wild look lit her eyes. She was still far above the ground. One slip and she'd plunge to the sidewalk with a terrible, furry *splat*!

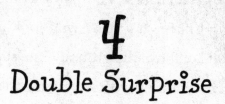

4
Double Surprise

Cody whipped into action. She pulled off Wyatt's exploding-alien T-shirt and stretched it like a net under a trapeze. Not a moment too soon! MewMew slid earthward. She gave the tree one last scritch-scratch, and then her paws shot out like Super-Cat. MewMew was in the air!

"Oh, no!" yelled Spencer.

Whomp! MewMew scored a direct hit on Wyatt's T-shirt. She was so heavy that Cody tumbled to the ground.

"Are you all right?" Spencer asked.

The cat's head popped out of the T-shirt. She looked pleased, as if defying death had turned out to be fun. As if she might consider doing it all over again.

"She's perfectly fine," said Cody. "Are you forgetting that cats have nine lives?"

"Thanks for saving her," he said. "I better go before Grandma Grace gets worried." He held out his arms for the cat.

They had just met, but Cody could already read MewMew's mind. That cat did not want to say *adios*.

"I'll walk you home," Cody said.

Spencer's grandmother lived just around the corner, on Cody's favorite street. All the houses were doubles. They had two of everything, side by side.

Two front doors. Two porches. Two mailboxes. It was like when you dribble paint on paper, fold it in half, then open it, and ta-da!

"That one's Grandma Grace's house." Spencer pointed.

The left side had tie-dyed curtains in the windows. Its front porch was cheery with a swing, wind chimes, and pots of flowers. On the right side, a skull-and-crossbones flag flew. That porch had a single rusty chair that had probably been there since dinosaurs roamed the earth.

"Thanks again." Spencer reached for MewMew, but Cody held on tight.

"I could hypnotize her for you," she offered. "So she won't ever run away again."

"Thanks anyway," he said.

Cody handed the cat over. MewMew gave a heartbroken cry. It was cat for "I'll miss you so bad."

Cody watched Spencer and MewMew climb the

front steps. It was no use hoping he'd open the door on the right side. Anyone could tell he wasn't the type to have a pirate grandmother. Still, as Cody turned away, lonesomeness threw its heavy arm across her shoulders. Just a little while ago, she hadn't even known that Spencer and MewMew existed. And now she missed them. In this life, there are many surprises, and not all of them are good.

"Cody!" yelled a voice. "Where are you?"

Wyatt came around the corner, wearing socks but no shoes. His eyes bulged in a googly, not especially attractive way.

"Yoo-hoo!" She waved her arms over her head. "Over here, *amigo!*"

Wyatt marched into the street without looking both ways. This was an enormous mistake, because he could have gotten hit by a car. Instead, he got hit by something almost as deadly.

Payton Underwood on her bike.

"Eeek!" Payton screamed.

The next thing you knew, they were down in a tangle of four arms, four legs, and two spinning wheels. If this was a movie, they'd stand up and brush each other off. They'd laugh and make swoony eyes and — *music, please!* — Kissing Time.

But in real life, Payton jumped to her feet and yanked Wyatt to his. His hair stood up like he was in the middle of a private hurricane.

"You should watch where you're going, Wyatt." Payton tossed her own silky hair. "Also, I suggest you try this new invention called shoes."

Payton jumped on her bike and rode away. Wyatt stared.

"She's so dumb!" Cody cried. "She didn't even ask if you were okay!" She felt his arm and leg bones. "Are you okay, Wyatt?"

Her brother looked at her. Just as a balloon fills with air, then suddenly pops, so did drooping Wyatt become exploding Wyatt.

"You left the house without telling me!"

"I was on a rescue mission!" Cody pointed across the street. "See that cat? Your T-shirt saved her life! If not for you—"

"Let's go home." Wyatt spun around, then started

hopping on one sock-foot. "Ow. Ow-ow. See what you did now?"

Cody knew that that particular rock being there at this particular moment was not her fault. But inside her, a wise voice whispered, *Do not argue at this time.* So she waved good-bye to Spencer and MewMew. Spencer waved back. Then he took MewMew's paw and made her wave, too.

Aw. That was so nice.

Cody caught up to Wyatt, who was limping. "Lean on me," she said, taking his arm. "I promised Mom I'd take care of you."

In reply, Wyatt put her in his famous, escape-proof headlock. As anyone with a big brother knows, this is what they do when really, truly, in their heart of hearts, they want to hug you.

5
Head of Shoes

Cody watched Wyatt do his body-building exercises. His skinny, powerful arms were ropes of steel! Afterward, he washed his face with his stinky soap, then switched on the computer.

Wyatt planned to be a surgeon. His favorite computer games involved internal organs. The screen lit up with squiggles and squished blobs. Wyatt clicked and dragged each one inside the outline of a human body. Humming, he put the liver, heart, and stomach exactly where they belonged.

Which is very important. But not that fun to watch.

"Where's the guts?" asked Cody. "Are those the guts?"

"*Silencio,*" said Wyatt.

Cody knew it wouldn't be long till she started begging him to please please please let her play My Darling Pets. To avoid bad behavior, she found a bag of chips and took it outside.

Just in time! Some foolish ants were marching toward the street and certain death. What a day for rescues! Cody had just scooped them onto a chip when her mother's car turned the corner. It was too early for Mom to be home. Something must be wrong. Cody dropped the ants inside the chip bag for safekeeping and ran to meet her.

Mom's cheeks were pink. Her eyes were unnaturally bright.

"Are you sick?" Cody asked. "Did you get the ax?"

"Big news. News the size of Texas."

Inside, Mom sat Cody and Wyatt down on the couch. She pressed her hands to her heart.

"Mr. O'Becker offered me a promotion. He offered to make me Head of Shoes!"

"Head of Shoes!" That cracked Cody up. She could just see it! Also a Foot of Hats! "Wow! That's great!"

"You rock, *mamacita*," said Wyatt.

Mom went up on her toes like a ballerina, but a second later came back down. "It's a trial period. After that, Mr. O. will judge my performance and decide if I get the job for keeps."

"*No hay problema*," said Wyatt. He grabbed the chip bag from Cody and began to munch.

"I don't know." Mom paced back and forth. "I've never been anyone's boss before."

Cody and Wyatt traded looks. That was news to them.

"I'll need you both to help me," said Mom. "Can I count on us pulling together? Will you be my support team?"

Group hug! Even Wyatt participated, meaning this was one extra-special occasion. Cody did a left-handed cartwheel. Life was good! For ambidextrous training, she tried a right-handed cartwheel and landed on her bungie. Life was still good!

"My trial starts Monday," said Mom. "The same day as your camp, Cody. I'll have to work extra hours, but you can go to Before-or-After-Camp."

Before-or-After-Camp! As if Now-Camp wasn't bad enough!

Even Wyatt looked upset by the news. A strange expression crossed his face. He hooked his finger inside his mouth. He pulled it out and stared at the shiny black blob on its tip.

Oh, no.

"I'm going to call Dad, then fix us a celebration dinner." Mom hurried to the kitchen.

Wyatt flicked away the black blob and followed her.

That left Cody all alone. Feeling terrible.

Terrible for her brother who'd just chomped ants.

Even more terrible for the ants who'd just gotten chomped.

In this life, one minute things are perfect, and the next you are an ant-murderer.

An ant-murderer headed for Before-or-After-Camp torture.

6
Dreams

"Cody!" said Mom. "Cody, wake up!"

Cody was dreaming that she held MewMew in her arms. Fat, sweet, deaf old MewMew. But when she opened her eyes, it was her pillow instead. The fog of sleep lifted. There stood Mom, clutching her ashtray.

Mom didn't smoke anymore. But when she got very upset, she cuddled her old ashtray. It helped soothe her.

Today was Monday, her first day trying out for Head of Shoes. She wore her black dress with the shiny red buttons, and her red patent-leather slingbacks. Not counting the ashtray, she was gorgeous.

"Camp's closed," Mom said.

"What?" Cody must have fallen back asleep without noticing. She was having the world's most beautiful dream.

"Your camp is closed. It's a toxic dump!"

"That's what I've been trying to tell you," said Cody dreamily.

"No." Mom paced up and down. "For real. The director sent an e-mail on Friday, but I only read it this morning. The playing field is giving off some kind of emissions. The whole place is shut down until further notice."

Click-click-clump. Mom stepped on Gremlin. Gremlin used to be Wyatt's, but now he lived in Cody's room.

"Thank goodness Wyatt's doctor camp doesn't

start till next week," Mom said. "You'll have to stay home with him."

Cody sat up and pinched herself. Ouch! This was no dream.

"I can't be late my very first day!" Mom bent to kiss Cody's cheek. Only she missed and got her in the eye. "I have to run."

Click-click-click, out of the room. Then *click-click-click,* back into the room.

"I know," said Cody. "No ants in the house, no screen time until—"

But now Mom sat down on the bed.

"Honey," she said, "this new job means a lot to me. But you and Wyatt mean much more! Maybe I should just stay home. I can call in. I'll say I'm sorry but this isn't going to work."

Poor Mom! She looked so upset. Cody scooted close and rubbed her mother's back in steady circles, the way the earth goes around the sun. She'd learned how to do this from Mom herself.

"We'll be fine," Cody said. "First days are always hard. But everything will work out. Just you wait and see."

"Oh, honey."

"You're the world's best mom. And you'll make the world's best boss."

"Oh, and you're the world's best girl." Mom gave a sniffle. "If I'm going, I better go. I hate to go. Here I go."

Mom kissed her again, this time right on target. Clutching her ashtray, she sped out of the room. Cody and Gremlin went to tell Wyatt the good news.

Deep asleep, he hugged his pillow tight.

"Payton," he murmured. "Oh, Payton."

Payton! Payton Underwood, a girl who had run him down with her bike and not even said sorry. Cody was in the nick of time.

"You're having a nightmare, Wy! Wake up! Wake up!"

Her brother's eyes flew open, then clamped shut.

"You are not here," said his robot voice. "You are at camp. I am having a nightmare."

"No way! I'll prove it!"

And Cody gave her brother's arm a helpful pinch.

7
Two for One

Wyatt was on the computer again. But instead of internal organs, today he was examining photos of other kids at parties.

Kids dancing. Kids laughing. Kids dancing and laughing at the same time.

Payton Underwood was in every picture. Her hair could be the star of a shampoo commercial.

"Guts are more interesting," said Cody.

Wyatt sighed. He clicked off and began his exercises. Over and over, he pulled himself up on his bar. His face went from carnation pink to stop-sign red. At last he let go and hit the floor. Cody followed him into the bathroom, where he scrubbed his face with his stink-bomb soap.

"That soap is a waste of money," she said. "You use it every day and still get loads of pimples."

Wyatt dried his face. He peered sadly into the mirror.

"Any more helpful hints?"

"I thought you'd never ask!" said Cody. "Let's go see MewMew."

"WhoWho?"

Outside, Cody fed the ants their afternoon snack. Then she dragged her brother down the street. By now, Spencer would be getting really lonesome. Just think! She got to make two people happy at once! Just like a store special: "Buy One, Get One Free."

On Spencer's porch, a short, cozy woman watered

the flowers. If she were a building, she'd be a cottage. Her pink T-shirt said I ♥ SCIENCE.

"I know who you are," she said. "You're Cody."

"Hello, Grandma Grace. This is my big brother, Wyatt."

"Call me GG."

GG's hair was a silver nest, only instead of birds, several pairs of glasses lived there. She set a pair on her nose.

"You're in the nick of time. Spencer's parents just called. They're extending their vacation an extra week. Poor pumpkin's got the blues."

"So does my brother," Cody whispered.

"Let's cheer them up," GG whispered back.

Inside, Spencer sat on the sofa with his hands in his lap and his feet on the floor, the student of every teacher's dreams. MewMew lolled around on the cushions like a plump naked lady in a museum painting.

"This is my brother," Cody told Spencer, "who's the same age as MewMew."

Spencer spoke not a word.

"A-choo!" went Wyatt. "A-choo!" But then he pointed at MewMew. "Look. It has its initial on its head."

How could Cody have missed it? Four lines formed a dark-gray M on MewMew's forehead.

"It's a monogram, like Mom has on her blue sweater!" said Cody. "MewMew the monogrammed cat!"

Wyatt sneezed some more. His nose ran. His eyes began to water.

"I'm allergic to the secretions of feline sebaceous glands," he said. "I'm having a histamine reaction."

"And how," said GG, handing him a box of tissues.

It turned out GG was a biology teacher at the high school. Wyatt perked up at that news. He told her he planned to be a surgeon. The two of them went into the kitchen together, discussing stuff you don't really want to hear about.

Cody pulled MewMew onto her lap and rubbed her monogram. Every cat has a secret purring switch, and she'd found MewMew's.

"GG's super nice," Cody said.

Spencer nodded.

"But you're still homesick," she said.

More nodding.

"Maybe you can have a teeny-tiny bit of fun. You know, in between being homesick."

"They were supposed to come," he burst out. "But they changed their minds. That's not fair! And Grandma Grace plays music too loud and cooks veggie burgers. And my pillow here is puffy, and at home it's flat. Plus the backyard has an extremely dangerous hole in it."

"Really?" Cody could hardly wait to see that. But Spencer's bottom lip was trembling.

"You've got the blues," she told him. "But your

parents will come before long. In the meantime, try to be brave."

Spencer shook his big, round head. A tear spilled over.

"What?" she asked. "You don't want to be brave?"

"I can't," he said.

"Just try, *amigo!*" she said. "Even ants can be brave."

"You think you know everything," he said.

Things were not going well in the cheering-up department. Too bad humans didn't have hidden purring switches you could flip. In this life, animals are superior in so many ways.

8
Quite a Week

At dinner that night, Cody and Wyatt told Mom about their day. She said, "Oh!" and "Cool!" and "I hope you said thank you!" in all the right places.

But when she told them about her day, it was a different story.

Head of Shoes was responsible for crabby customers. For example, the woman who tried on thirty-two pairs of shoes and didn't like any. Or the man who demanded fur-lined boots even though it was June.

"Another woman went to a party in a pair of our jeweled gladiator sandals. Her boyfriend stepped on her foot while they were dancing and broke her toe."

"That's not your fault," said Wyatt.

"I tried to tell her that," Mom said. "But Mr. O'Becker gave me a lecture. He said the customer is always right, even when she's wrong."

Mom's lips puckered, like she'd bitten something rotten. At times like this, Cody could tell that being a grown-up was harder than it looked.

"To make matters worse, your camp is closed for good, Cody. And every other camp I called is full," said Mom. "What are we going to do when Wyatt's doctor camp starts?"

"I'll come to work with you," Cody said. "I'll tell those cranky old customers to just get over it."

"I need to lie down," said Mom. "I've got the whim-whams."

. . .

It was quite a week for everyone. GG's house had lots of books about blood and brains for Wyatt to enjoy. Music was always playing, and GG was happy to demonstrate dances like the Mashed Potato, the Hustle, and Saturday Night Fever. Out back, her half of the yard had a vegetable garden and chairs shaped like butterflies. The other half looked like someone was trying to tunnel to China.

"Grandma Grace says the kids next door have been digging that hole forever," said Spencer. "Sometimes they even dig in the middle of the night."

Those kids were away on vacation. Or maybe in reform school. One afternoon, Cody and Spencer built a contraption that fired rocks into the hole. Spencer said its proper name was a catapult.

It worked with marshmallows, too. Also eggs from GG's fridge. Though Spencer only let Cody do that once.

Oops. Twice.

Oops. Once more.

At home, Spencer said, he never played outside. At home, his house was climate-controlled. He had his own computer. Also his own personal flat-screen TV.

"Sounds to me like you're spoiled," said Cody.

"Sounds to me like you're jealous," said Spencer.

"I challenge you to a staring contest," said Cody.

Using her special blurring vision, Cody was the easy winner. Spencer pretended not to mind.

"You don't know everything," he said.

"Nobody does," said Cody. "Except Wyatt. The only thing he doesn't know is how to make Payton Underwood fall in love with him."

"Payton Underwood?" Spencer cocked his head. "You mean her initials are P.U.?"

"P.U.!" Cody smacked her forehead. "You're right!"

That cracked Cody up. It cracked her up so bad, she fell over backward and rolled around on the grass.

"Pee-yoo!" she gasped. "Peeeee-yooooo!"

"It's not nice to laugh at other people," Spencer said.

Then he made a tiny *plip* sound, like one drop of milk in a glass. *Plip-plip-plip,* went Spencer, faster and faster, till that glass of milk was full to the brim and overflowing. By then Spencer was laughing so hard, he rolled around on the grass, too.

The two of them crashed into each other and then, somehow, they rolled into the hole. Since the hole contained catapulted rocks and smashed eggs, this should not have been a fun experience.

But it was.

Even for Spencer.

9
The Twang of the Heart

All week long, Mom left early and came home late. Search back through the mists of time, and you would not find a shoe salesperson who worked as hard as Mom.

Saturday was O'Becker's busiest day. When Cody woke up, she heard her mother getting ready to go. Jumping out of bed, she ran for a good-bye hug. But when she burst into the kitchen, Mom spun around and gave a gasp.

"Oh, dear," she said, hiding her hand behind her back.

"What's that?" Cody tried to see. "A surprise?"

It was a surprise, all right. Mom was holding a pack of cigarettes.

"You quit!" cried Cody. "You promised to never coat your lungs in filthy black tar again!"

"I wasn't going to actually smoke them," said Mom. "I was just going to look at them now and then. When the whim-whams got really bad. But that was a mistake."

Mom was wearing her best outfit, the gray pants suit and imitation snakeskin stilettos. Now she tapped the garbage pail with her imitation snakeskin toe. The lid flew up. The cigarettes flew down.

"There." She dusted her hands together. "Close call. Thank goodness. Oh, my. What was I thinking?"

You might suppose a kid would enjoy being 100 percent right and having her parent admit it. But you would be wrong.

"Dad comes home tomorrow," Mom said. "It's my day off, and we'll have a nice cookout. Okay?"

"Okay."

Mom kissed Cody good-bye. Cody slowly buttered her toast with her left hand. She carefully wrote Wyatt a note with her right hand. Outside, early as it was, the ants were already hard at work. Cody lay down on the sidewalk for an ant's-eye view. Did they ever get the whim-whams? They had plenty to worry about. For example, human foot-stompers. Or enemy ants. But there they were, working away as hard as ever. As Cody watched, they touched their eyelash-thin feelers. That was ant for "Keep your spirits up, old buddy!" She tore her toast crusts into extra-tiny pieces for them.

Down the street in the neighbor's front yard, a baby skunk snuffled the grass. Skunks weren't supposed to be out in the daytime. Its white stripe went only halfway down its back. This was a beginner skunk, and it didn't have the hang of things yet.

A vine of tenderness climbed up inside Cody. Oh, how she longed to pet that pointy little head! But inside her, the wise voice spoke. *Put your hand in your pocket*, said the voice. *Pet that sweet stink-machine with your eyes alone.*

So Cody walked on, around the corner to the seeing-double street. Spencer sat on the porch swing, not swinging. He was still wearing his pj's. They were so faded, it was hard to tell what the pictures on them were. Elephants, maybe. Possibly toasters. His sturdy wrists and ankles stuck out.

"Those pj's are your old favorites, aren't they?" she said.

"My mom threw them away, but I rescued them," he said.

"Moms really need our help sometimes."

Spencer pushed his glasses up his nose. He plucked at a toaster/elephant.

"When I try to help my parents, they say, 'Spencer dear, you're getting in the way.'"

"Too bad for them," said Cody. "In my opinion, you could be a very helpful person."

"Probably that's why they didn't take me on their trip. Because I'd get in their way."

Very gently, Cody started the swing swinging.

First Mom and her cigarettes.

Then the ants.

The baby skunk.

Spencer's worn-out pj's.

In this life, so many things can twang your heart.

If only she and Spencer had feelers, she'd have touched his right now.

"My dad is coming home tomorrow," Cody said. "We're having a cookout, and you should come."

He bit his lip. Decisions were hard for Spencer, even no-brainers. Cody sped up the swing a teeny-tiny bit, to help him make up his mind.

"Will you have veggie burgers?" he asked.

"My dad hates those," said Cody.

"Okay," Spencer said at last.

"Hooray! MewMew can come, too!"

Oh, no. There he went, thinking again. Cody made the swing go a little faster.

"What if she gets scared and runs away again?" Spencer asked.

"Did you forget? I'm going to hypnotize her. I will put her in a light trance, and
then . . ." Cody snapped her fingers, only
they didn't snap. She tried her other hand.
Oh, well. "MewMew will never run away
again."

"Have you hypnotized other cats?"
he asked.

"What a question!" she said.

"Whenever my parents hire someone, they check references. That way
they know the person is dependable."

Spencer's parents didn't sound so
hot in the dependable department, if
you asked Cody. But did she point this
out? No. Instead, she went straight to
the heart of the matter.

"I know I can do it," she said.

Half an inch! That's how close he

was to being convinced! But Spencer had one last question.

"How do you know you can if you never did it before?"

Cody stopped the swing so fast, their heads thunked against the back.

"The lining of your gut replaces itself every three days," she said.

"What's that got to do with—"

"Wyatt explained it to me. Your body makes new cells around the clock. It throws the old ones out. Right this instant, you're manufacturing new skin and toenails!"

Spencer examined his toes.

"You're not the same Spencer you were five minutes ago," Cody said. "Part of you is brand-new and improved! You might have all-new, undiscovered talents!"

Spencer folded his hands in his lap.

Cody waited.

She decided they were elephants.

She wondered if that baby skunk had gotten home okay.

She hoped Mom was having a good day.

Just when she was about to give up on him, Spencer whispered, "Okay."

10
The Hypnotists

Late that night, Cody woke up. Her Dad radar was beeping. She raced to the kitchen. Dad sat at the table with Mom. Jumping into his arms, Cody breathed in great gulps of Dad smell—a mix of diesel oil, coffee, and eggs over easy.

"Little Seed!" he said, cuddling her up. "How are things in the petunia patch?"

Cody told him all about Spencer and GG and MewMew. Holding her close, Dad hung on every word.

Next thing she knew, she was waking up in her bed, morning sun spilling through her windows. Cody pulled on her clothes. Mom and Dad's bedroom door was shut. When he came home from a haul, they required their personal privacy.

In the kitchen, Cody stuck a banana in her pocket. She clapped Dad's cowboy hat on her head and wrote a right-handed note.

WENT TO GG. HOME SOON WITH SUPRISE GESTS.

Wow. Her right-handed writing was getting quite excellent.

Spencer waited on the porch with MewMew. He wore a pair of enormous sunglasses. He looked ready to brave an attack of mutant aliens armed with deadly lasers.

"I want to make sure I don't get accidentally hypnotized," he explained.

For some reason, this made Cody slightly nervous. She peeled her banana and ate it extra slowly. Her mouth got that dried-up, after-banana feel.

"Let's go in the backyard," she said. "It's too distracting out here. MewMew and I need to concentrate."

"All right."

In the back, Cody gazed down into the amazing hole. She tugged on the brim of Dad's hat. She scratched a mosquito bite on her ankle. She plucked a blade of wet grass off her big toe. Wow, now that bite really itched. She scratched some more.

"You're not stalling, are you?" asked Spencer.

Teachers say there are no stupid questions. But teachers are not always correct.

"Please hand me the subject," Cody said in a voice of command. "Then fetch a blanket and a glass of water."

Spencer handed over MewMew, then ran inside. In Cody's arms, MewMew lay sound asleep, paws tucked up. If this worked, she could bring MewMew home. Cody couldn't bring her inside, since Wyatt was allergic. But she could make a cozy cat-bed under the tree. And feed MewMew tender morsels from her own plate. It'd be the next best thing to having a real pet of her own. If only it worked!

Spencer came back with a bedspread printed with swirly designs. Cody instructed him to spread it on the grass. Holding MewMew with one hand, she drank the water with the other. Then she took off Dad's hat and handed it to her assistant.

Lying on her back, she settled MewMew on top of her.

"Look into my eyes." Cody made her voice deep. "You cannot hear, but you can understand. You will obey us, MewMew."

MewMew stretched her neck and yawned. Cody yawned back. Having a cat this big on top of you was like being crushed beneath a thousand fuzzy blankets.

"You are growing sleepy."

MewMew gazed at Cody. Cody gazed back at MewMew. MewMew's eyelids drooped. Cody's eyelids drooped back.

"Hear our command, O great scaredy-cat," said Cody. "You will never run away again. You will stay close beside your beloved masters. Forevermore."

Cody crooked a finger at Spencer.

"Touch her ears," she whispered. "To make sure she receives the command."

Spencer touched a gray ear, then jerked his hand back.

"Did you feel something?" Cody asked. "A tingle? A small shock?"

Spencer nodded.

"MewMew, you may awake," commanded Cody. "Or, okay . . . you may continue to sleep."

Cody slid the cat onto the bedspread and sat up. Spencer removed his giant sunglasses.

"Did it work?" he asked in a voice of hope. "Did we really do it?"

Till this minute, Cody had concentrated on how wonderful it would be for *her* if hypnotizing worked.

But now she looked deep into Spencer's eyes. And she got a surprise. Cody saw how wonderful it would be for him, too. If it worked, Spencer would know that when he truly tried, he could do new and amazing things.

Cody covered her eyes. All this gazing into other eyes was making her dizzy.

"You think we did it?" Spencer repeated. "Do you? Are you sure?"

Cody put her hands down. She looked at Spencer, and she nodded. Slowly, bit by bit, his round face lit up like a birthday cake. He looked so nice, you wanted to make a wish on him.

11
Perfect

"Far out!" said GG when they asked if Spencer could go to Cody's house. "I'll get a jar of my green-tomato chutney and walk you right over."

"MewMew's invited, too," said Spencer.

GG raised her eyebrows. She tapped her bottom lip.

"You don't need to worry." Spencer stuck out his chest. "She won't run away. We hypnotized her."

"Is that so?" GG rummaged in her hair and found

a pair of glasses. She put them on and looked at Mew-Mew, who was back asleep. "It's hard to tell."

"The lining of your gut replaces itself every three days," said Spencer. "You never know what new talent you might develop."

"I can't argue with that," said GG. "Tell you what. Let's put her in the cat carrier."

You could smell Cody's house half a block away. Dad had his big smoker fired up. He took his hat off Cody's head and put it on his. Then he took it back off and tipped it to GG. He said he'd heard all about her, and the next time she was having a dance party, he wanted to come.

Mom invited GG to stay for the barbecue. But GG said it was nice for Spencer to do something all grown-up and independent. And Mom said ah, she got it. And then they exchanged smiles of secret, grown-up understanding, and GG went home.

Overhead, the sun was a big yellow beach ball on a bright-blue blanket. Cody set MewMew's carrier in the shade of the maple tree. She unlatched the door, but MewMew stayed inside.

Wyatt did chin-ups on a tree branch. He chased Spencer and Cody with the hose. He even gave Spencer a lesson in the Houdini headlock.

"The angle of the elbow is all-important," he said, grabbing Cody. "The victim is rendered helpless."

Spencer nodded gravely. "There's some kids back home I could use that on."

Mom carried out bowls of potato salad and coleslaw. For a practically once-in-a-lifetime

treat, she gave them cans of pop. It was hard to believe, but Spencer had never shot root beer out his nose.

"There are more useful things to teach a person," Mom said.

But then she kicked off her hot-pink espadrilles. *Wiggle-wiggle* (her toes). *Smile-smile* (her mouth).

Cody did a left-handed cartwheel. She did a right-handed cart-wheel—and for the first time in her long life, she didn't fall on her bungie!

There are days that should never be.

And then, there are days that, oh, if only they could go on forever!

While they ate, Cody felt something fuzzy on her foot. A something way too heavy to be a caterpillar. She ducked her head under the picnic table.

Mew? said MewMew. *Mew mew?*

That is cat for "May I join you?"

Cody set MewMew on the bench and fed her bits of burger.

Dad said, "Call the zoo. There's a wild animal on the loose."

Mom said, "I'd love a dress the same green as her eyes."

After a while, MewMew jumped down into the grass. Cody and Spencer watched her sniff and explore. They could

hardly breathe. This was The Test.
What if something scared her?
Would she run?

MewMew tenderfooted her way
toward the maple tree. All at once,
a blue jay squawked. Like a tiny
fighter jet, it zoomed over
MewMew's head.

The cat coiled tight, a big furry ball in a slingshot.

Then, *boing!* She leaped, spun in midair, and dove under the table, where she huddled on Cody's foot.

Cody looked at Spencer.

Spencer looked at Cody.

In perfect sync, they raised their palms and high-fived.

"It worked!"

If this were a movie, everyone would hug, music would swell up, and ta-da! Happy Ending Time. The whole audience would burst into applause.

Only this was real life.

Where things are not so simple.

At all.

12
Two Things

Dad had three more days off, so Cody got to stay home with him.

Is there any need to say how wonderful that was?

But the day before he was due back on the road, two things happened.

Neither one was in the Happy Ending category.

Thing #1: Wyatt fainted at doctor camp.

When camp called, Cody and Dad jumped in the car and sped there. Wyatt sat in the nurse's office, his face like an uncooked marshmallow.

"Are you all right?" cried Dad.

The nurse had brown eyes and a kindly smile. She said, "It's common to faint when they do their first dissection."

At the word *dissection*, Wyatt leaned his head against the wall.

"He'll be fine," said the nurse. "But you better take him home for the rest of the day."

In the car, Wyatt sat with closed eyes. Cody knew what dissection was. She'd watched her brother do it online. You cut open a once-alive creature, and then you removed its internal organs. Watching made her stomach feel like a blender on high. But if she ever said "Ack," or "Ugh, that is so gross," Wyatt called her a fainthearted, weak-kneed girl.

"What did you dissect?" Cody asked from the backseat.

"An earthworm," croaked Wyatt.

Cody gulped. Worms were not in her top ten of the animal kingdom. But still.

"I would never do that," she said.

"Surgeons have to do it," said Wyatt. "If you can't dissect, you can't be a surgeon. End of story."

This was bad news, all right.

Dad cleared his throat. Some grown-ups give so much advice, you don't need to listen. You can be sure plenty more is on the way soon.

But not Dad. His advice was rare and precious as golden coins.

"Wyatt, when I drive my rig down that lonesome highway, I pay attention to what's in front of me," he said. "But at the same time, I keep my eyes on what lies up ahead. I see the big picture."

"Uh," said Wyatt. "Okay."

"It's the same on the Road of Life," Dad went on. "You have hit a pothole here. You have hit a traffic jam. But you can't focus on that. The road stretches before you. Keep your eyes on the many miles that lie ahead."

He pulled up in front of the house and said he was

going to the grocery store. Inside, Wyatt collapsed on his invisible bed. Thinking of his life as a road full of potholes wasn't helping.

But before long, Dad came back with all of Wyatt's favorite foods. He heaped a plate with chips and dip and filled a bowl with moose-tracks ice cream.

"I have another surprise," Dad said as Wyatt began to eat. He turned to Cody with a grin. "I figured out what to do with you, Little Seed!"

Thing #2: Dad hired a kid-sitter.

It got even worse.

"I saw an ad on the store bulletin board. I called and spoke to the world's nicest girl. She has lots of experience. She even offered to give me references! She's just your age, Wy."

Wyatt's mouth was too stuffed with chips to reply.

"In fact, she knows you," said sunbeam Dad. "Her name is Payton Underwood."

Wyatt started choking. Dad pounded him on the back. Slimy chip bits landed on Cody's arm.

"Payton?" Wyatt sputtered. "Here? In our house? With Cody?"

"What?" Dad looked concerned. "Is something wrong with her? Payton, I mean?"

In this life, what grown-ups don't know can be astonishing.

"She's the girl of his dreams," Cody told Dad in a low voice. But not low enough.

"She is not!" howled Wyatt. "But you have to call her back and say she can't come."

"Too late for that," said Dad.

"You have to! Right now! It'll be too embarrassing! It'll ruin my life!"

"You! What about me?" Cody flicked a slimy chip bit off her arm. "I'm the one who's getting a hard-hearted shampoo commercial for a sitter. You think that's going to be any fun for me?"

"This is definitely the worst day of my life," said Wyatt. "This day will live in infamy."

"Besides," said Cody, "did you just call me embarrassing?"

"Is the sky blue?" said Wyatt. "Do bears poop in the woods?"

"Go easy," said Dad. "It's going to be all right. Cody will behave." He rested his hand on top of her head. "I can count on you. Right?"

"You can count on me. But possibly not some other people around here."

Dad's talent was giving magic hugs. When you were in the magic middle of one, you magically felt kind toward the whole world. You magically couldn't stay mad at anyone or thing for long.

Even a brother who called you embarrassing.

Because probably he was still faint-brained. With no idea what he was saying.

13
P.U.

When Cody woke up the next morning, Dad was already gone. But he had left a note on her pillow.

Dear Little Seed,

Take care of Wyatt and Mom. I'll be back soon.

Big buckets o' love,

Dad

When Mom poked her head in the doorway, she was holding her ashtray.

"I miss him already, too." She heaved a sigh. "To

make things worse, Mr. O'Becker asked me to come in early today. *Asked* me, ha-ha!" She walked down the hall, laughing way too loud. "As if!"

Poor Mom. The whim-whams were winning. Cody found her markers. She turned over Dad's note and drew a red circle. In the middle she wrote her message, then made a fat red slash across it, like those signs for No Smoking.

In the kitchen, she found Mom's big work binder and slipped the note inside.

Today was turning out to be the Day of Notes. Another one lay on the table.

Cody, Act normal or suffer a slow and painful death. W.

Click-click-click. Mom came into the kitchen wearing her electric-blue dress and her silver sandals with kitten heels. She'd just poured her coffee when the doorbell rang.

"You must be Payton," said Mom. "Right on time!"

Payton wore a red sundress and sparkly flips. She and Mom admired each other's outfits. Then Mom gave her a quick tour of the house and a list of five hundred emergency numbers. Payton nodded and smiled.

"I kid-sit all the time?" She made it sound like a question.

"Wyatt should be home around five," said Mom. "I'll probably be late again. We start inventory today."

"Wow," said Cody. "Are you going to invent new shoes?"

Mom and Payton laughed merrily. It was like they were instant best friends!

Mom gulped her coffee and grabbed her binder.

"I'll call at lunchtime."

And then it was just the two of them.

"I have to feed the ants," said Cody.

"All right," said Payton.

She pulled out her phone and began texting.

She was still texting when Cody came back inside. Cody narrowed her eyes.

"You're popular, aren't you?" she said.

"Me?" Payton looked surprised. "I wish?"

Payton smelled delicious. She smelled like a recipe Mom made with apricots, cinnamon, and chicken, only without the chicken. Cody sniffed her own hair. Nothing.

I have boring hair, she realized.

"So you're Wyatt's little sister?" said Payton.

"How come you say everything like a question?" said Cody.

Payton's cheeks got rosy. "It's a bad habit? I mean, a bad habit. I'm trying to break it? Break it."

"I used to suck my thumb," said Cody.

"Oh, me too! And twirl my hair at the same time."

Payton had a toe ring. It was a silver dolphin with a twinkly green eye. She let Cody try it on. She said it looked so perfect, Cody could have it.

"You have really long toes," Payton said. "My aunt says that's a sign of intelligence."

It was getting harder by the minute to dislike Payton Underwood. But then Cody reminded herself: this girl had broken Wyatt's tender heart.

"Too bad my big brother's not here," she said. "He's at doctor camp."

"Really?" Payton looked amazed. "I might want to be a doctor? But I got a D in science this year."

"That's just a pothole on life's long highway," Cody told her.

Payton's phone rang. While she talked, an idea planted itself in Cody's brain. It grew super fast, like that bean in "Jack and the Beanstalk." By the time Payton hung up, the idea was so big, it practically lifted off the top of her head.

"There are some things I'd like to show you," she said.

"All right," said Payton.

In the bathroom, Cody held up Wyatt's anti-pimple soap.

"He uses this every day. He is very clean."

Payton's mouth did a funny little twisty thing. Next, Cody showed her Wyatt's exercise bar.

"He works out every day. Ask him to show you his muscles."

Next stop on the Tour of Wyatt was the computer.

"He sits here for hours each day," said Cody. "You may not have noticed, but he is a genius. If you want someone to help you get an A+ in science, Wyatt is your man."

Payton sat down in the chair and twirled it around. Apricot and cinnamon perfume spun out on the air.

"Your brother seems nice," said Payton. "Too bad he's so shy. Everybody calls him Quiet Wyatt."

"Quiet!" said Cody. "He's not the least bit quiet! He'll talk your head off if you let him."

"One thing I so hate is a show-off," said Payton.

"Show-off!" said Cody. "The last thing he is is a show-off!"

"I like in the middle. Not too shy, not too conceited," said Payton.

"The middle!" said Cody. "That's exactly where Wyatt is!"

Now she had to sit down, too. Convincing someone to fall in love really took it out of you.

When Wyatt got home later, Payton gave him a big smile. Wyatt got very interested in his shoes.

"We so had a great day," she told him.

"Okay," he told his shoes.

"Your little sister's like the world's funniest and cutest. She adores you?"

"Huh."

"Well, I better get going."

Out of conversation, Wyatt just nodded.

When Payton was gone, he opened the fridge and stared into it so long you could practically watch his hair grow.

Cody wiggled her toes. If you did this just right, the dolphin on the ring looked like it was swimming.

"Payton is interested in you," she said.

Wyatt spun around. His face wore the same naked-baby-bird look as Spencer's when he took off his glasses.

"She didn't say that," he said. "She said that?"

He started to put her in a headlock. But then he changed his mind. Instead, he poured them both tall glasses of chocolate moo-juice. And even though it wasn't quite exactly perfectly five o'clock, he let Cody play My Darling Pets on the computer.

You might think, What a nice way to end the day. And you would be right.

Except it was not the end of the day.

14
A Most Embarrassing Incident

By the time Mom came home, Wyatt and Cody had already eaten half the mac and cheese they'd made to surprise her.

"What a day!" she said. "First inventory. Then a most embarrassing incident."

"Poor Mom." Cody patted her arm. "Did you fart? Or bump into a display like I did last time I came to work with you, and all those running shoes fell down like a shoe blizzard?"

"No," said Mom. "Not that." She opened her work binder. "This."

She held up the note Cody had made that morning. There was the big red circle, with the words CRABBY CUSTOMRS and MEAN OLD WHIM-WHAM MR. O. in the middle. And there was the fat slash through it all. It looked so professional, Cody felt a surge of pride.

"You found it!" she said.

"No," said Mom. "Mr. O'Becker found it when he was checking my binder."

"Oh." Cody felt herself shrinking. Shrink-shrink-shrink, till she was mouse size. "That was not the plan," she squeaked.

Wyatt took the note and busted out laughing.

"OMG," he said. "This is *excelente!*"

"I'm glad someone thinks it's funny," said Mom.

But then the corners of her mouth curved upward. She pulled them back down, but *sproing!*

"His face!" Mom said. "You should have seen the man's face!"

And then she started laughing, too. She leaned back and laughed till her arms got all dangly. Cody hated to be left out, so she did some fake laughing, which is even harder than fake crying. But then Mom pulled herself together.

"Lucky for you, Cody Louise, Mr. O. has children and grandchildren. He was upset at first, but he got over it. I think."

"I was trying to help," said Cody.

"I know." Mom put a scoop of mac and cheese on her plate. By now it was all gluey, but Mom ate it anyway. "From now on, promise me you'll think things through before you act."

"You mean like Spencer? He thinks and thinks till you want to bop him one!"

"I'm not talking about Spencer. I'm talking about you." Mom held up her fork like a pointer. "I know you meant well. But it's possible to do the wrong thing for the right reason."

That made Cody's brain sputter. What was Mom talking about?

But Mom's fork was still in the air. "Do you promise?"

In this life, some questions are not questions. And the answer to them is always "Okay."

15
Love Magnet

Payton Underwood was a love magnet.

When Cody opened the cat carrier, MewMew trotted straight to her and licked her hand. When Payton sat down, the cat curled up in her lap. Payton rubbed her monogram, and she purred like a miniature lawn mower.

"Usually she's a shy scaredy-cat," said Spencer. "Like me."

Payton tilted her head. "Scaredy-cat?" she said. "You? You look way brave to me."

Boom. He was in love, too.

When it was time to go inside for lunch, Mew-Mew was sound asleep under the maple tree.

"Should we bring her in?" asked Payton. "She looks so peaceful, I hate to disturb her."

"No need," said Cody. "She won't go anywhere."

"She's hypnotized," said Spencer. "We did it."

"Really?" said Payton. "You're just one surprise after another!"

Spencer gazed up at her with swoony, love-struck eyes. It was enough to make you lose your appetite, except that Payton fixed peanut-butter-and-marshmallow sandwiches.

Cody checked on MewMew every few minutes. On and on that cat snoozed. A butterfly landed on her and fluttered its wings. That is butterfly for "What a large and furry rock!"

When Spencer and Cody went back outside, Mew-Mew stood up, stretched, and sat on Cody's foot.

"She's hypnotized, all right," said Spencer in a voice of joy.

Payton brought them Popsicles. Her phone sang its little song, the way it did every two minutes.

"Yo, *Michael*," she said, flipping her hair.

Pause. Hair flip.

"Oh, *right*? Like I believe *that*?"

Pause. Hair flip.

"Keep *talking*, why don't you?"

Payton giggled.

"Be *quiet*, why don't you?"

Which, if you were paying attention, was the exact opposite of what she'd just said.

Not that it mattered.

Worry began to nibble Cody's insides. What if blabbermouth Michael had really big muscles instead of beginner muscles, like Wyatt? What if he used soap that smelled good instead of like old dead fish? What if Payton fell in love with him instead of Wyatt?

Cody got so worried, she forgot all about her Popsicle till a chunk fell on her toes.

"Follow me," Spencer told MewMew. "I command you, O faithful cat."

He walked backward, and MewMew followed him. He walked sideways, and MewMew followed him.

"You are in my power," he said. "You will do my bidding forevermore."

MewMew stuck out her tongue and licked his Popsicle.

If this were a cartoon, at that very moment a lightbulb would have flashed over Cody's head.

Because suddenly she knew how to make Wyatt's dream of love come true.

It was so simple. Why hadn't she thought of it before?

But wait.

She'd promised Mom that from now on, she'd

think things through before she acted. And if anyone kept her promises, it was Cody.

What could go wrong? She tried to wiggle her stuck-together toes. If the plan didn't work, things would stay just as they were. Which would be too bad, but not a disaster. That was the worst that could happen. Right?

Ta-da! Her toes unstuck. The dolphin on her ring leaped for joy. Cody ran to tell Spencer the plan.

16
The Worst That Could Happen

"You're not going to make me croak whenever I hear the word *frog,* are you?" asked Payton. "Or scratch like a chicken every time I see corn? I saw that on YouTube."

"No way," said Cody. "We take hypnotizing very seriously. Right, Spencer?"

"Right," he said.

If only he'd stop taking off his glasses and putting them back on, as if he hoped that next time he looked, he'd see something different.

What he saw was: Payton lying on the swirly bed-spread on the grass. With her head on Wyatt's pillow with its X-Men pillowcase.

"This pillow smells like a chemistry experiment," she said.

Cody didn't explain that was a combination of Wyatt's anti-pimple soap and his own one-of-a-kind self. It was important that the subject be relaxed, with a clear and open mind.

"Please hand over your cell phone," said Cody. "We cannot be interrupted."

"Yike-ster," said Payton. "You guys *are* serious."

"Please." Cody turned to her assistant. "Cue the calming music."

Spencer turned on Wyatt's iPod and set it beside Payton's ear.

"I love this song," said Payton.

Overhead, the leaves of the maple tree rustled softly. The scent of honeysuckle drifted on the air. Payton yawned. She slid her feet out of her sparkly flips.

"Oh, wow," she said, and yawned again. "I was up late last night. If I'm not careful, I'll fall sound asleep."

Spencer and Cody looked at each other. It was already working!

"You are slipping into a light trance," Cody said softly. "Do not resist."

"Umm." Payton snuggled into Wyatt's pillow and sighed. "Ooookay."

"We may be misusing our power," Spencer whispered.

"The two of them are meant for each other!" Cody whispered.

"Maybe we should think about this some more," Spencer whispered.

"Too late!" Cody whispered.

"What are you whispering about?" Payton whispered.

"Nothing," they whispered together.

Next door, a sprinkler gently swished. The tiny iPod voice sang, and a bird up in the maple tree joined in. Payton made a sound like a sweet piglet rolling in mud. Cody bent closer, examining the subject. Payton was snoring!

"I'm not sure. . . ." began Spencer, but Cody gave him the zip-lips signal. She turned off the music.

"Payton Underwood, hark to our command," she said. "When you wake, you will remember one thing. One thing and one thing only."

Payton's eyelids fluttered. Cody pointed a your-turn finger at Spencer.

"Umm," he said. "Uh. Umm." His shoulders smooshed up around his ears. "You do it," he told Cody.

"When you wake, you will be in love," said Cody. "You will love someone who has loved you faithfully and truly, lo these many years."

Payton lay still as a statue. She was ready. Ready to receive their command!

"When you wake," said Cody, "you will be in love with my brother, Wyatt."

"Wyatt?" Payton rocketed to life. "Wyatt's in love with me?" She said this the same way you'd say, *Martians are landing on my roof right this minute?*

"Uh-oh," said Spencer. He jumped up and backed away.

"How can Wyatt be in love with me?" said Payton, her cheeks growing rosy. "I so hardly know him!"

It seemed possible Payton hadn't been in a trance after all.

"Uh-oh," said Spencer, louder this time.

He began to peek under bushes. Then he disappeared inside the garage. He was trying to hide! He was pretending that this whole thing was Cody's idea and that he'd had nothing to do with it! Some friend he turned out to be!

"Wyatt?" Payton could not stop saying his name. "I never dreamed?"

"Oh, well, never mind." Cody tried to change the subject. "How about Popsicles all around?"

"Who'd have guessed in a million years that Quiet Wyatt was in love with me?"

A sound like a person getting swallowed by a boa constrictor made them turn. Guess who stood behind them, his eyes googling out in a not especially attractive way? Guess whose jaw hung open so you could probably see his tonsils if you went a little closer, which you definitely, absolutely would not want to do at this moment?

Ding ding ding, you win! It was Wyatt, home from doctor camp.

In this life, there are moments when the earth might as well open up and swallow you right down, because you are already doomed to death.

But then that traitor Spencer said, "Uh-oh!" one more time. And his voice held such heartbreak and desperation, they all looked at him.

"What's wrong?" cried Payton.

"MewMew!" said Spencer. "She's gone!"

17
Even Worse

Even though she was deaf, they shouted her name.

"MewMew!" That was Wyatt.

"MewMew, where are you?" That was Cody.

"MewMew, come back!" That was Spencer.

Payton said she was sorry? But she had to go home?

"Ha," said Wyatt after she left. "She obviously wants to get as far away from me as possible."

Cody waited for him to say this was all her fault. Or maybe he'd skip talking and get straight to strangling her. But instead, Wyatt kicked a rock. Then another one.

"Who cares about Payton, anyway?" he said.

"You," said Cody sadly. "And I'm really, really sorry. I wanted to hypnotize her the same way we hypnotized MewMew, but . . ."

But they hadn't really hypnotized MewMew, either. They just thought they had. And then they'd forgotten her, and something must have scared her, and she'd run away. And who knew where she was now, frightened and confused and lost? And old and deaf and not exactly very smart?

Cody's insides felt crumbly. It was like she was lost, too, even though she was standing in her own backyard.

When Wyatt hooked an arm around her neck, she braced for the headlock. But instead, he pulled her close.

"We'll find that *gato*," he said. "I promise."

Magic happened. He was still Wyatt, but for a moment, he was Dad, too. Cody mashed her face against his T-shirt and held on tight.

But then she remembered Spencer and turned around.

He stood there, looking so miserable that she felt lost all over again. But then . . .

"It's your fault!" He shook his finger in her face. "You act like you know everything! But you don't! You're just a big fat faker!"

His words were poison arrows flying through the air. Ouch! Ouch!

"You don't know how to hypnotize!" Spencer said. "You tricked me! And now MewMew's lost! She's in mortal danger!"

Cody opened her mouth, but nothing came out. Her voice was broken.

"I will never be your friend again!" howled Spencer. "I wish I never met you! Never! EVER!"

"Hey, go easy," Dad-Wyatt said. "This is no time for fighting. We have to pull together. We need to think like that cat. Where would she go if she ran away?"

Cody and Spencer locked eyes. Two brains, one thought. Just like that, they both began to run.

Cody was faster than Spencer. She sped down the street. If only, if only! By the time she got to the pine tree where she'd found MewMew that very first day, Cody could hardly breathe. She threw her arms around the trunk and peered up into the branches.

An annoyed squirrel peered down at her.

Cheee! it said, which is squirrel for "No way, José."

Spencer and Wyatt raced up, faces full of hope. But Cody only shook her head sadly.

"We better tell GG," said Spencer.

Climbing GG's front steps was like going up Mount Everest with hundred pound weights on your feet. GG had raised MewMew from a tiny kitten. They'd belonged to each other longer than Cody had been alive!

GG was wearing her yellow TO LIVE IS TO DANCE T-shirt. But when she saw their faces, she didn't look like dancing.

"Bummer," she said. "What happened?"

"MewMew's lost!" Spencer blurted out. "She ran away!"

"Oh, no." GG rummaged for her glasses, even though she was already wearing a pair. "Oh, dear."

Cody hung her head. Every poison-arrow thing that Spencer had said was true. This was all her fault.

GG put a hand on Cody's shoulder. She put the other one on Spencer's shoulder. She was a GG bridge, linking them together.

"MewMew is a scaredy-cat," GG said. "She won't go far. She'll find someplace good and safe and wait till we find her."

Cody peeked at Spencer, but he refused to look back. Part of her thought, *I don't blame you for being mad at me.* But another part thought, *Who needs you, anyway, you old sniffle-puss?* And that was so confusing, she decided to stop thinking for a while.

GG said they'd hunt around here. Wyatt promised to call later. Then Cody and her brother walked home slowly, eyeballing every shrub and lawn chair and parked car. They asked one person after another if they'd seen a fat, striped cat. "No, sorry," they all said.

By the time they got home, Mom was there. When she heard the news, she quick-quick changed from her kitten heels to her neon-green walking shoes. Just before they fanned out over the neighborhood, who should ride up on her bike but Payton Underwood.

"I feel so responsible?" she said. "And besides, I adore that cat. Can I help look?"

Even though Mom, an official grown-up, stood right there, Payton looked at Wyatt. He cleared his throat several times, like he was about to make an important speech in front of an enormous crowd.

"Sure," he said.

18
The Search

Wyatt went left, Payton went right, and Mom and Cody went in between. Cody looked up into every tree. She checked behind garbage cans and on strangers' porches. The world is full of hiding spots. You could never imagine how many till you searched for a cat.

At the corner, Cody froze. Something squished lay in the road. Her heart began to beat too fast, and her throat closed up. She reached for Mom's hand.

MewMew was so slow. And deaf. And clueless. What if . . .

Mom checked. "A squirrel!" she said.

Whew. Cody felt sorry for that run-over squirrel, she really truly did. But oh, thank goodness it wasn't MewMew!

At last, Mom said, "It's too dark to see. And you haven't had any dinner."

Dinner! Cody would never eat again. But by now, her eyes and ears were playing tricks on her. Every shape was a cat shape. Every sound was a cat cry. It was getting hard to put one foot in front of the other. When they got home, Payton and Wyatt were waiting on the front steps.

"I just talked to GG," he said. "They didn't find her, either."

"Not yet, that is," added Payton.

What if it wasn't *ever*?

Payton twirled a ribbon of hair and pooched her lips.

"Wyatt called the animal warden," she said. "He's going to post MewMew on the Lost Pets website, too." She gazed at him with eyes of admiration. "He's thought of everything."

"*No hay problema.*" Wyatt flexed his arm, making a muscle.

Payton laughed. Then Wyatt laughed. Even Mom laughed. Laughed! At a time like this! Cody couldn't believe it. Furious, she rushed past them, up the steps and inside. In her room, she grabbed Gremlin and hugged him tight.

Gremlin was made of rubber, so you could cry on him forever and he didn't get soggy.

Mom came in. She held out a peanut-butter-and-marshmallow sandwich.

"I'm not hungry," said Cody.

"You're not giving up, are you?" said Mom.

Cody hugged Gremlin.

"Because that wouldn't be the Cody I know," Mom went on. "The Cody I know always has a new idea. And she always tries again, even if she makes mistakes. Not only that, but she believes in giving people another chance. She's a friend to all, even ants. Today at work, I thought of that girl. Mom, I told myself. Mom, take a lesson from Cody."

Cody sat up. "For real?"

"And you know what? Today was my best Head of Shoes day yet. Even Mr. O'Becker said so."

Cody sank down. "But now MewMew's lost."

"Tomorrow's a new day."

Grown-ups have to say things like that. No

grown-up who walks this earth is allowed to tell a kid, Tomorrow may be just as bad as today, and guess what else? It may be way worse.

But now Mom put her arms around Cody and rubbed her back in slow, steady circles, just the way the earth goes around the sun.

"Eat your sandwich, sweetie," she said. "You'll feel better."

Cody knew she wouldn't. But she managed a couple of bites, and then Mom helped her get ready for bed.

19
The Kingdom of Night

Cody lay listening to the night. A dog barked. A siren *whup-whupped*. A baby cried. In the dark, each sound stood out by itself. It was so different from daytime, when they all mushed together.

Was Spencer asleep? Or was he lying awake, wishing he'd never met her? Heavy as an iron pot, that's how Cody felt. A pot filled with sadness stew.

She climbed out of bed and tiptoed down the hall

to Wyatt's room. She longed to wake him up to keep her company, but he'd only get mad. Besides, she remembered at the last minute, *she* was mad at *him*.

So she just leaned in the doorway a little while, then tiptoed to the kitchen. She opened the back door and slipped outside.

A lot was happening in the Kingdom of Night. White-winged moths fluttered around the porch light. Fireflies blinked secret messages. Hidden in a tree, a bird sang a silvery solo. The grass rustled with creatures too small and sly to be seen. Up above, the man in the moon smiled down on it all.

Cody climbed onto the picnic table. How nice it was out here, in the pale glow of the almost-full moon! It made you wish you were an owl swooping or a spider spinning, at home in the mysterious darkness. Daytime was boring by comparison.

But now Cody's eye fell on something beneath the maple tree. For a moment, she couldn't figure out what it was. Then all at once, she knew.

MewMew's carrier.

Spencer had left it there.

The night's wonderfulness folded its wings and flew away. That empty carrier was the saddest thing Cody had ever laid eyes on.

Now she knew what Mom meant about doing the wrong thing for the right reason. She'd meant to help Wyatt and Spencer, but instead she'd embarrassed her brother, made her friend hate her, and lost the world's sweetest cat.

That bird began to sing again, but now its song was sad and lonesome. *Oh, no,* it sang. *I'm all alone in the night. Oh, no. Oh, no.*

Creak! Cody jumped and almost toppled off the table. But it was just Wyatt, opening the back door. Yawning and rubbing his eyes, he climbed up on the table next to her. He didn't ask Cody what she was doing. Instead, he put her in a headlock.

It felt so good.

But suddenly he stiffened.

"What's that?" He pointed.

An animal was tenderfooting its way across the dark yard. It stopped to sniff the grass, then trotted toward the carrier. They watched it crawl inside.

"It looked like a raccoon," said Wyatt. "It probably wants MewMew's cat treats."

They crept toward it.

"Careful!" Wyatt held out an arm. "Raccoons can carry rabies, which is an acute disease of the nervous system!"

But then he reared back.

And gave a mighty sneeze.

20
The Sweetest Thing

She was back! Sweet, scaredy-cat MewMew had found her way home.

While Wyatt ran to tell Mom, Cody cradled her close. Her fur was stuck with bits of burr, and her nose dabbed with mud.

"Where were you?" Cody asked. MewMew tried to reply, but for once, Cody couldn't translate.

"You don't seem hurt." Cody rubbed her monogram. "You seem *excelente!*"

Mom hurried out in her powder-blue satin

bedroom slippers. Like a rock star, MewMew let them adore her.

"We have to tell Spencer and GG!" Cody said.

"It's midnight," said Mom. "They're asleep."

"I bet they're not," said Cody. "Please, Mom!"

So they put MewMew inside her carrier and walked down the street in the moonlight. But as they got closer, Cody got nervous. What if Spencer didn't forgive her? After all, she hadn't exactly found Mew-Mew. The cat had found her own self. Cody hadn't

done any rescuing. What if Spencer still called her a big, fat faker?

"Hey!" said Wyatt as they turned the corner. "Their lights are on!"

"They're on the porch," said Mom, and began to wave. "Guess what?"

GG and Spencer rocketed off the swing.

"Look who's here!" cried GG. She gave Spencer a bear hug. About half a second later, Cody got one, too.

In GG's kitchen, the kids had cookies and moo juice. Mom and GG had cookies and wine. You practically needed a ticket to get a turn petting MewMew. Cody explained how MewMew had strolled up out of nowhere, as if to say, What's the big fuss?

Then GG told how she and Spencer tried to sleep but gave up. Spencer, wearing his elephant/toaster pj's, nodded.

"This is the latest I ever stayed up in my entire life," he said.

"Well," said GG with a chuckle, "you've done a lot of things you never did before since you and Cody became friends."

Cody slid down in her chair. Did GG mean that as a compliment? Or something else? Besides, they weren't friends anymore.

Mom stood up. "I have to get to bed. Tomorrow's the final day of my trial." Her forehead did its folding-fan imitation.

"And tomorrow I have to dissect"—Wyatt swallowed hard—"a frog."

So far, Spencer hadn't said a single, solitary word to Cody. But now he followed her outside.

"Maybe it really did work," he said in a quiet voice.

"What?" Cody turned around.

"She came back. All by herself. Maybe MewMew really is hypnotized."

"I didn't think of that," said Cody. A little fountain of happiness bubbled up inside her. She began to picture all the other people and animals she could hypnotize. But then she shook her head. "We better not take any more chances. It's too risky."

"I never thought I'd hear you say that," said Spencer.

"Right. Well, I guess I better go."

"Wait. I was thinking."

Is the sky blue? Cody almost said. But the wise voice inside her said, *Be quiet.*

"Maybe MewMew wasn't lost," Spencer went on. "Maybe that first time she ran away — that time it was my fault and you found her in the tree—maybe she liked it, and she wanted to do it again. Maybe she's not really a scaredy-cat after all. Maybe down deep, she's brave and adventurous! Maybe"—he stopped for breath—"maybe I'm really sorry I said all that mean stuff to you."

Inside Cody, the fountain of happiness shot sky high.

"I'm sorry I said I knew how to hypnotize," she told him. "I just wish I did. Only not anymore. I'm sick of hypnotizing, to tell you the truth. And from now on, I'm going to think before I act. Not for a gazillion years, like you, but long enough to make sure I don't do the wrong thing for the right reason. Or the right thing for the—"

"Cody Louise!" called Mom. "Come on!"

Cody sighed. She was worn out, but in a very nice way.

"I'll see you tomorrow," Spencer said.

"It is tomorrow," said Cody.

"You act like you know everything," he said.

High above, the stars winked. The man in the moon smiled down. *Hush-hush* went Mom's slippers on the sidewalk. *Swish-swish* went Wyatt's baggy shorts.

In this life, many things are sweet. But that night, if Cody had to name the sweetest thing of all, it would be walking in the summer moonlight, with her mother holding one hand and her big brother holding the other.

21
Not Even Cody

Before she went to sleep, Cody wrote two notes. She tucked one inside Mom's binder and one inside Wyatt's bike helmet. Then she climbed into bed and catapulted into a delicious sleep.

In the morning, Payton was so happy to see Mew-Mew that she took photos with her phone. Then she posted them on the computer and showed Cody and Spencer.

She scrolled quick-quick past all the pictures of popular kids laughing and dancing. And then ta-da!

MewMew sleeping.

MewMew looking out the window.

MewMew sleeping.

MewMew poking her toy.

MewMew sleeping.

MewMew with Cody's finger pointing to her monogram.

MewMew sleeping.

MewMew had special, one-day-only permission to be inside the house. Sleepy from staying up so late, Cody and Spencer watched a movie with Mew-Mew snoozing between them. Outside, it began to rain. If you think that was cozy, you are 100 percent correct.

"Pretty soon I have to go home," Spencer said.

Cody nodded. GG was throwing a party to celebrate MewMew's adventure. Everyone was invited, even Payton. They were going to dance the night away! They planned to raise the roof!

"I mean home home," said Spencer. "My parents are picking me up in a few days."

Once, going home was all he wanted. But now Spencer's face got very complicated. Sadness and gladness were mixed together.

Sometimes when you look at another person, it's like looking in a mirror.

"I just remembered something!" Cody said. "You never met my pet ants."

"You mean pest ants?"

Cody fetched crackers and an umbrella, and the two of them went outside. It had been days since Cody had visited the ants, and she knew they'd be glad to see her. She and Spencer crouched down by the curb.

Not an ant in sight.

"Hello," she said. "It's me!"

Rain tapped the umbrella. It dented the tops of the ant volcanoes. Oh, no. What if they thought Cody had abandoned them? Even worse—what if something had wiped them out?

"Hello? Hello?"

She should have known! Nothing defeated the ants! Two popped up. They touched feelers, then ske-daddled across her toes. They touched feelers again and skedaddled over Spencer's foot.

"They like you!" Cody told him. She crumbled up the crackers, and they watched the ants work together to drag a monumental piece back to the colony.

"I'm going to tell my parents I want to come back," said Spencer.

"Really?" Cody did not trust her ears.

"Before the end of the summer, I'll be back. *Amiga.*"

Spencer smiled a brave smile. He looked so nice, Cody touched her forehead to his and did a little rub-a-dub-dub.

Spencer laughed. And then he did it back.

Later, after MewMew and Spencer had gone home, Cody and Payton decided to watch the rest of the movie. They'd just settled onto the couch when footsteps pounded up the front steps. Wyatt burst in, hair glued to his head. Raindrops dripped off his nose.

"I did it!" He punched the air like he'd won the Olympics. "I dissected a frog!"

"Oh, wow!" said Cody. "You didn't faint this time?"

"Faint?" Payton tee-heed as if Cody had made a joke. "Like Wyatt would ever faint!"

Wyatt shot Cody a look that said *I-will-make-you-faint-if-you-tell.*

"Oh, right," said Cody. "Tee-hee."

But now Payton pointed her finger at Wyatt's dripping nose.

"How could you do such a thing?" she demanded. "I am opposed to dissection. I am opposed to anything that involves animal cruelty."

"Surgeons have to dissect." Wyatt rubbed his dripping nose. "Are you opposed to surgeons?"

"I'm going home to get ready for the party." Payton flipped her hair. "If you think I'm going to dance with you, you can think again."

And she marched out the door.

Wyatt rubbed his head. "That girl gives me a brain pain."

"Hey," said Cody, "that's my job!"

While Wyatt took a shower, Cody curled up on the couch. The rain let up, and sunlight the color of lemonade spilled across her toes. Cody's eyes drooped, and she was in a beautiful dream. Payton and Wyatt were dancing the Mashed Potato together. GG was laughing. MewMew stood on her hind legs and danced, too. For once Mom came home early, just in time. . . .

"I'm ready to party," said Mom.

"Umm," said dreamy Cody. "I know."

"Open your eyes and see a surprise," said Mom.

"Huh?"

When Cody opened her eyes, real-life Mom was sitting right next to her. Pinned to her dress was a name tag edged in gold. SUPERVISOR, FOOTWEAR DEPARTMENT, it said.

"Mom! You're Head of Shoes!"

"I am!"

Now Wyatt wedged himself onto the couch, too. He smelled like some new, nonstinky soap. When Mom heard he'd done his dissection, it was group-hug time. This was even more pleasant than usual, since Wyatt smelled so good. And then it was Mom's turn to tell about her day.

"When Mr. O. called me into his office, he looked so serious I was sure it was bad news. So I decided to be honest. I told him how at first, I hadn't been sure I could manage the job."

Mom picked up her purse and set it on her lap.

"I said what kept me going was my family. I showed him the note I found in my binder today." She opened her purse and pulled it out.

Even if I have a new gut, my hart is always the same and it loves you.

"Hey," said Wyatt. "I got one of those, too."

Cody held her breath. She'd meant well! Only by now she knew meaning well was no guarantee.

But Mom broke into a smile as bright as her new name tag.

"Mr. O. said I certainly have an unusual family. I said he was certainly right. Then he said the number-one requirement for a good supervisor is handling a million things at once. And then he said I was the one for the job!"

Group Hug, the Sequel!

Mom called Dad to tell him all the good news. While they talked, Cody leaned back. She admired Mom's new pin and Wyatt's new smell, and she thought of her new friends, and the millions of new cells her body was making, and how tomorrow was a new day and who could tell? Who knew what wonders it might bring?

Nobody.

Not even Cody.

Acknowledgments

My fountain of gratitude bubbles over with thanks to Sarah Davies, and to Liz Bicknell, Carter Hasegawa, and everyone at Candlewick Press. Thank you, Ohio Arts Council and the Vermont Studio Center. And to all the teachers, librarians, and booksellers who have been so kind to me and who do so much for young readers — a little ant rub-a-dub-dub.

From the first day of summer vacation through fall and winter to long-awaited spring, there's a full year of adventure for Cody and her neighbors!

"Springstubb creates a kind of magic in these books, with their gentle humor . . . and real empathy for kids struggling to figure out how to do the right thing."
— *The Buffalo News*

www.candlewick.com